THE RABBIT
WHO
WANTS
TO FALL
ASLEEP

✤ A NEW WAY OF GETTING CHILDREN TO SLEEP ✤

THE RABBIT WHO WANTS TO FALL ASLEEP

CARL-JOHAN FORSSÉN EHRLIN

ILLUSTRATED BY IRINA MAUNUNEN

ACKNOWLEDGEMENTS

Thanks to all of you who shared your knowledge and time to make this book a reality:
Eva Hyllstam, Matt Hudson, Nadja Maununen, Irina Maununen, Lisa Sjöberg,
Matina Rendahl, Siv Duvling, Kevin Shearman and my beloved wife, Linda Ehrlin.

LADYBIRD BOOKS

UK | USA | Canada | Ireland | Australia
India | New Zealand | South Africa

Ladybird Books is part of the Penguin Random House group of companies
whose addresses can be found at global.penguinrandomhouse.com.

ladybird.com

Penguin
Random House
UK

Originally published in Sweden by Ehrlin Förlag as *Kaninen som så gärna ville somna* in 2010
Kaninen som så gärna ville somna copyright © 2010 by Carl-Johan Forssén Ehrlin
Subsequently published in the English language by CreateSpace Independent Publishing Platform,
North Charleston, South Carolina, USA, in 2014
Published by agreement with the Salomonsson Agency

This edition published in Great Britain by Ladybird Books 2015

001

Printed and bound in Italy

A CIP catalogue record for this book is available from the British Library

ISBN: 978–0–241–25516–2

INSTRUCTIONS TO THE READER

Warning! Use this book with caution. It may cause drowsiness or an unintended catnap. And never read this book out loud close to someone driving any type of vehicle or engaged in any other activity that requires wakefulness!

The author and publisher very much hope your little one falls asleep, but make no guarantees and can take no responsibility for the outcome!

The Rabbit Who Wants to Fall Asleep is intended to help children fall asleep more easily at home or in school. For best results, the child should use up excess energy before listening to the story. Sometimes the child needs to hear the story a few times before he or she can relax completely and feel comfortable. Take your time to read this book and use your best fairy-tale voice. Also make sure you are not disturbed while reading. By following these simple guidelines, you will create the best environment for the child to relax, feel calm and fall asleep. The content in this book is based on powerful psychological techniques for relaxation, and it is recommended that you read the story from the beginning to the end, even if the child falls asleep before you have finished reading. It is best if the child is lying down while listening, instead of looking at the pictures, so that he or she can relax even more.

Feel free to read the story in a normal manner to get used to the text, before using the reading instructions recommended below. Then use the different techniques and see how the child responds.

- **Bold text** means you should emphasize that word or sentence.

- *Italic text* means you should read the word or sentence with a slow and calm voice.

- In some parts of the book you are asked to yawn or give a physical action. These parts are marked as ***[action],*** or ***[name]*** where you read the child's name.

- The name of the rabbit, Roger, can be read as "Rohhh-gerrr" with two yawns.

This book contains specially constructed sentences and choices of words. Some can appear a bit unusual in the text; they are intended to be that way since they have a psychological purpose. If you find it difficult to read the story as recommended, *The Rabbit Who Wants to Fall Asleep* is also available as an audiobook. This may be more beneficial for the child, and you can also enjoy listening to this book together, while the child falls asleep and perhaps even you, if you desire to do so.

Be well and sleep well!

Carl-Johan Forssén Ehrlin

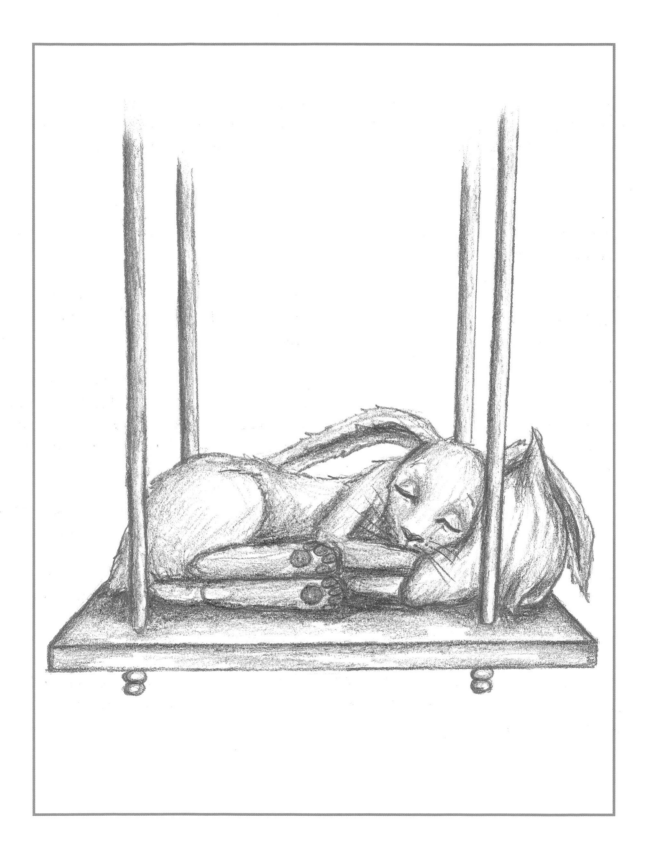

I am going to tell you a story that can make you feel very sleepy. Now, some people can fall asleep straight away while others wait a little while until you drift off to dreamland. *[Yawn]*, *[name]*, I'm wondering just when will be the best time for you to go to sleep – now, or before the story ends . . .

Once upon a time, there was a little rabbit called Roger, who really wanted to fall asleep, **and could** not, **right now.**

Roger the Rabbit was just your age. Not older, not younger, exactly as old as you are, *[name]*. He enjoyed doing all the things you like doing, to play and have fun. He would rather stay up and play all evening instead of **sleeping, now.**

All of his siblings **easily fell asleep every evening** when Mummy Rabbit tucked them into bed, but not Roger the Rabbit. *He was just lying there* thinking of all the other things he wanted to do instead of **going to sleep, now.** How he could be outside, playing on the grass, and just run around, until he got so tired, *so tired that he could not run around any more.*

Roger could play in the park all day long until he fell asleep on the swings. *Now. It allows him to swing back and forward, back and forward, slowly and relaxing.*

The rabbit began **feeling even more tired** when he thought about all the games he would play and **how tired that would make him now**, before his mummy would say, "Hush Roger, and **sleep, now.**"

All the sounds he could hear made him and you, *[name]*, even more and more tired. He was about **to fall asleep**; he did not know how soon. **Now.** How **close to sleeping** he really is. How the picture of him and you sleeping becomes clearer and closer with every breath, **now.**

This very night Roger's siblings **fell asleep quicker than usual**, while he was lying there **thinking about falling asleep, now**. He was lying there thinking about all the things that can make him **tired now**, all those things that usually would make him *tired and sleepy, so tired and sleepy. All the playing, all the sleeping and all the other things that would cause him and you to be tired, right now.*

These things did not help Roger the Rabbit, so he decided to do something about it. Daddy Rabbit was sleeping, but Mummy Rabbit was still awake, so Roger went to talk to her. She suggested that he and you should take all the thoughts that are lingering in your head and put them in a box by the bed.

"Tomorrow when you wake up, you will have the answers to all your thoughts and you will be filled with energy, but **now, you will fall asleep**," said Mummy Rabbit with certainty in her voice.

"Sometimes it takes a little longer, but you will always receive an answer to the thoughts you put in your box," said Mummy Rabbit. Roger and you are doing this, now. It feels very relaxing and peaceful to be free in your mind and be ready to fall asleep.

Afterwards, she suggested they would go together with you to see Uncle Yawn, who was the world's kindest wizard and who lived just on the other side of the meadow.

"This will, **with all certainty, help you both to fall asleep**," said Mummy Rabbit.

So you all agree to go and see Uncle Yawn, who would help you fall asleep, now. On their way through the door, Roger the Rabbit thought of all the times Uncle Yawn had helped him before. He had made Roger and **you fall asleep** using his magic spells and magic sleeping powder so many times before, and this would happen even now.

Since Roger was certain that he would fall asleep, he told you, [name], it is OK to fall asleep now, before the story ends. Because he knows that it has a happy ending and that you will both fall asleep.

Well on your way, Roger and you were *getting even closer to falling asleep*. You followed the little path down, *down* to Uncle Yawn. The path *down* that he knew so well. He had walked there many times before. *Just walked down, down and down . . . That's right . . . Good.*

When Roger the Rabbit and Mummy Rabbit had walked for a while, they met the kind Sleepy Snail with his house on his back.

"Where are you off to now?" asked Sleepy Snail curiously.

"*I am going down* to visit Uncle Yawn," said Roger the Rabbit, "because he will help me **fall asleep now**. How do you **make yourself fall asleep**?" asked Roger.

After a pause with relaxation, the kind Sleepy Snail said that the secret is to calm down and to do everything more slowly. *Walk slowly, so slowly. Move slowly, so slowly. Think slowly, breathe slowly and calm, slow and calm, just slow down now.*

"**It always works for me**," said Sleepy Snail.

"Thank you, I will try that," said Roger the Rabbit.

The kind Sleepy Snail said to you, *[name]*, **you will fall asleep to this story, so you can easily. Now. Allow yourself to fall asleep.**

Roger left Sleepy Snail and continued to walk into sleep.

"Thinking about lowering your tempo, as Sleepy Snail told us to do, seems like a good idea," Roger said.

He started to walk *slower and slower* and took smaller steps. *At the same time he started to breathe deeper and slower, he felt even more tired and felt how relaxing it is when things go slower. Roger got more tired, and the more he relaxed and calmed down, the more tired he and you became now, and the more tired and the more he relaxed, the more tired he and you became, now* **[yawn]**. *That's right.*

Roger and Mummy Rabbit *continued slowly* on the little path *down* to Uncle Yawn on the other side of the meadow. After a while, they met the beautiful and wise Heavy-Eyed Owl. She sat on a small branch next to the path that led *down* to Uncle Yawn.

"Hello, Heavy-Eyed Owl. Since you're a wise owl I would like to get help **to sleep now**. Can you help me?" said Roger.

"Of course I can help you to **fall asleep now**," answered the wise Heavy-Eyed Owl. "You don't even need to hear me finish talking, **you can already see yourself fall asleep**. *You feel calm and relaxed and can do as I tell you. Now. Fall asleep.* It's all about being able to **relax**. **Now, lie down.** In a little while, I want you to **relax** in different parts of your body. **It's important that you do as I tell you and just relax**," she said.

Since Heavy-Eyed Owl is wise, I will do what she tells me to, thought Roger.

Relax your feet, *[name]*. Roger and you do as Heavy-Eyed Owl tells you and **now you relax** your feet.

Relax your legs, *[name]*. Roger and you do so, **now**.

Relax your entire upper body, *[name]*. Roger and you do so, **now**.

Relax your arms, *[name]*. *Allow them to be heavy as stones.* The rabbit and you do so, **now**.

You are relaxing your head and allowing **your eyelids** to be heavier, *[name]*, just letting them relax. Roger and **you are relaxing deeply**. **Now.** You are letting your eyelids be as heavy as they are, *just before you fall asleep, now.*

Then Heavy-Eyed Owl said, "Let your whole body be heavy. So heavy that it feels like it **falls down** into the ground. *Fall down, down, down.* Just like a leaf that falls down, *slowly down, down, down, slowly down* from a tree, follows the wind, and *just let it make you fall down, slowly down* to the ground. *Slowly down, down, down. Now. Your eyelids are so heavy.*"

"This was good," said Roger, *now feeling how tired he had become. Very tired. Now. So tired that you almost fall asleep [yawn].* **Just as calm as it feels before you fall asleep, now.**

Roger the Rabbit had decided to go down to Uncle Yawn, so he continued to go down, *even though he was very tired, now*. Roger thought about what Sleepy Snail taught you, to walk *slowly and be calm to become even more tired*.

Roger **noticed how tired he was** and all he wanted to do was lie down and fall **asleep**. But I can't **lie down here, now, and sleep,** Roger the Rabbit thought. Besides, I have promised Mummy Rabbit that we will **go down** to Uncle Yawn and fall asleep, **now.**

After walking for a while, they reached Uncle Yawn's garden. Outside the house there was a big sign that said, **"I can make anyone fall asleep." Yes, that's true**, you now thought. **I feel even more tired already. Now. He has made me sleepier** with his spells, you thought.

When they reached the door, there was a little sign. It said, "Knock on the door when you, **now, are ready to fall asleep**." Roger felt tired and decided that **you are ready to fall asleep, now.** He knocked on the door.

Uncle Yawn opened the door and was happy to see you, Roger and Mummy Rabbit.

"Welcome, my friend," said Uncle Yawn. "Apparently, you would like some help to **fall asleep now."**

"Yes," answered Roger *[yawn]*, **"I would like us to fall asleep, now.** Both me and you, *[name]*."

Uncle Yawn took out his big, thick book that contained a lot of spells that can make both rabbits and humans **fall asleep**, be happy, be kind, be loved and feel that they are good enough just as they are. "Just like you can, are, and can be right now," said Uncle Yawn. He also took out his **powerful, magical and invisible sleeping powder** that makes rabbits and children fall asleep when it is sprinkled over them.

"When I now cast this spell and sprinkle the invisible sleeping powder over you, it is important that you will walk straight home and go to bed immediately. **Now. You will fall asleep already** on your way back **or in bed**. This spell and sleeping powder are powerful and always work, and **you will fall asleep quickly, now**."

"Finally, I can **fall asleep and sleep well all night**," said Roger with certainty.

"OK, I will now read to you," said Uncle Yawn, and he started to read the powerful spell that **would make** Roger and **you fall asleep, now**.

[While you count, symbolically sprinkle the invisible sleeping powder over and around the child.]

Three . . . two . . . one . . . sleepy now, sleepy now, I am sleeping now . . .

"Now it is best that you leave," said Uncle Yawn, "because you can fall asleep very soon! Your eyelids will become heavier and heavier, and you will get more and more tired with every breath you take on your way home, and you will realize how easy it is just to let go and fall into sleep. You will also fall asleep faster and sleep better every night in the future. Fall asleep better every night," said Uncle Yawn to you. "It doesn't matter if your eyes are open or, now, closed. It will only make you twice as tired."

Both of you now yawned *[yawn]*, thanked him politely, and walked home with Mummy Rabbit.

He thought to himself, How will I be able to walk all the way home without *falling asleep? I am so tired and want to go to sleep now [yawn], so tired I wish I was in bed now, listening while the sounds around me whisper sleep now. All the sounds slowly drift away. Now. When you fall asleep, Roger said.*

They started walking, step by step, your legs got heavier and heavier. So tired, so tired, just like Uncle Yawn had told you, tired you become now, tired you become, now.

After a while, they met the beautiful and wise Heavy-Eyed Owl again. Heavy-Eyed Owl told Roger the Rabbit, "I can see that **you are tired,** *[name]*, and that both of you are **very close to falling asleep, now**."

Roger **was very tired** and slowly nodded his head, said yes, and felt how right Heavy-Eyed Owl was.

I am well on my way to falling asleep now, you thought.

"**Goodnight**," said the wise Heavy-Eyed Owl. You are now **shutting your eyes and yawning yourself to sleep** *[yawn]*.

Roger the Rabbit continued home to his bed. Now. *More and more tired with every step.* He was longing for his warm comfortable bed and to be able *to sleep there just as comfortably as you are doing right now, sleeping comfortably, now.* The more Roger thinks about his bed, the more *tired he becomes now and the more tired he is,* the more he longs for his bed back home, which makes him and you *twice as tired. Now. You can fall asleep anytime.*

After a little while, they met the kind Sleepy Snail again, with his house on his back. Sleepy Snail had hardly got anywhere since last time they met. He is very slow, thought Roger, so he **must fall asleep easily now**.

Sleepy Snail was sleeping, and *barely noticed* when Roger the Rabbit passed him.

"You will also fall asleep soon, won't you?" said Sleepy Snail.

"Yes, I am so tired, all I want to do is shut my eyes, now. I can see myself falling asleep," Roger answered to Sleepy Snail. *Now. Continue to go deeper into sleep and also allow yourself to close your eyes again and fall asleep **[yawn]**.*

Roger the Rabbit was now *so tired* he could barely lift his feet any more, *so tired, so tired.* But still Roger and you, **[name]**, continued home and *even deeper into sleep, now.*

"With every breath, I am becoming *more and more tired,*" said Roger to himself. *More and more tired.* Soon I am at home, *so tired you cannot keep your eyes open any more.*

With every breath, the *eyes get heavier and heavier and shutting them now **[yawn]**. The eyelids are heavy as stones, heavy, heavy, so heavy.*

Roger the Rabbit saw his home. Finally, thought the tired rabbit, who is twice as tired. Now. We will both fall asleep and sleep well all night, **[name]**.

Roger arrived at the door and was so tired that he could not open it. This is how tired we are now, thought Roger, and yawned **[yawn]**.

Once inside, he saw his siblings and Daddy Rabbit *lying in their beds sleeping well. Roger walked slowly to his bed to sleep. Now. So tired, so tired [yawn]*.

Once in bed, he thought about what Uncle Yawn had said: Tomorrow you will both *fall asleep even faster and sleep even better, as you do now.*

Mummy Rabbit tucked him in gently and said **goodnight** to you, *[name]*, who **is very tired now** *[yawn]*.

"Yes, tomorrow you will *fall asleep even faster* – what a relief," said Roger to you and again *closing your eyes to sleep well.*

Now when Roger has fallen asleep, it is your time to sleep as well, as he is doing right now. Since Roger the Rabbit can fall asleep, so can you, **now**.

Goodnight.

ABOUT THE BOOK AND THE AUTHOR

You have read the book *The Rabbit Who Wants to Fall Asleep*. The book is the first in a planned series of children's books. Its intention is to help children sleep well, understand their own value, and be prepared to overcome obstacles in their life.

My goal with this book is to help all parents out there who are struggling with getting their children to sleep at night or naptime during the day. I want this book to help children relax and fall asleep faster every time they hear the story.
– Carl-Johan Forssén Ehrlin

Carl-Johan Forssén Ehrlin is a behavioural scientist with a bachelor's degree in psychology and teaches communications at a Swedish university. He is also a life coach and leadership trainer. Carl-Johan has combined all these skills and experiences in developing the techniques in this book. Read more about the author at carl-johan.com.

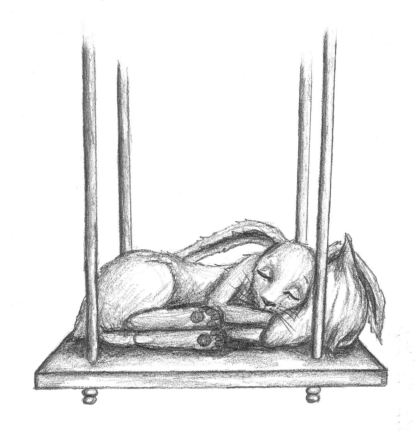